For Mike,
who always encourages
me to keep reaching

Farrar Straus Giroux Books for Young Readers
An imprint of Macmillan Publishing Group, LLC
120 Broadway, New York, NY 10271

Copyright © 2019 by Aidan Cassie
All rights reserved
Color separations by Embassy Graphics
Printed in China by Toppan Leefung Printing Ltd., Dongguan City, Guangdong Province
First edition, 2019
1 3 5 7 9 10 8 6 4 2

mackids.com

Library of Congress Cataloging-in-Publication Data

Names: Cassie, Aidan, author, illustrator.
Title: Little Juniper makes it big / Aidan Cassie.
Description: First edition. | New York : Farrar Straus Giroux, 2019. |
Summary: A little raccoon dreams of growing taller but, through a series
of events, learns to accept herself just the way she is.
Identifiers: LCCN 2018035809 | ISBN 9780374310455 (hardcover)
Subjects: | CYAC: Size—Fiction. | Self-acceptance—Fiction. | Raccoon—Fiction.
Classification: LCC PZ7.1.C443 Li 2019 | DDC [E] —dc23
LC record available at https://lccn.loc.gov/2018035809

Our books may be purchased in bulk for promotional, educational, or business use.
Please contact your local bookseller or the Macmillan Corporate and Premium Sales Department
at (800) 221-7945 ext. 5442 or by email at MacmillanSpecialMarkets@macmillan.com.

Aidan Cassie

Little Juniper Makes It BIG

Farrar Straus Giroux • *New York*

Juniper was little. *Too little*, she thought.

"Adults only build things in adult sizes," she grumbled just loud enough for her momma to hear. "If kids made houses, we'd make them so they fit properly."

Like all clever children, she found **unfairness** most annoying.

"Patience, Junebug," her momma said.

"You're growing more every day."

But three days later, Juniper
was *still* no bigger.

At bedtime she couldn't concentrate on her book. *For my whole entire life, everything's been too big for me,* she thought.

car seats

counters

Later that night, Juniper's little thought grew.

By breakfast, her little thought had become
a big idea. By lunchtime, a cunning plan.

Juniper assembled springboards and stilts,

built heighteners and hoppers,

made cranes
and catapults,
and . . .

... even flew by balloon.

But, despite her inventiveness,

Juniper's efforts **fell short**.

By Monday, Juniper felt smaller than ever.

Things were better at school. At school, she didn't feel little. At school, she was average.

Some kids were taller, and some smaller.
The new girl, Clove, was tiny.

Juniper liked hanging out with Clove. She was amazing. Being small didn't stop her at all.

"Sweet salamanders! How did you do *that*?!" asked Juniper.

"Grippy sharp nails, a parachute tail, and"— she lowered her voice—"extra-stretchy armpit skin. You want to come for a sleepover?" she asked. "We could practice climbing."

"Oh, YES!" said Juniper. Some un-smallness lessons were just what she needed. She counted the days until the weekend.

On Friday, Juniper packed her suction-cup shoes, thirteen feet of rope, and a helmet. She said good-bye to her momma and headed to Clove's house.

But when she arrived, she found she didn't need to climb or stretch for anything.

In Clove's home, Juniper was adult-size.

This house is perfect, thought Juniper.

Well, mostly perfect.

Hide-and-seek was
unexpectedly quick.

Swinging was
surprisingly slow.

And dress-ups were . . .

just awkward.

By the time they got ready for bed,

Juniper didn't feel small—at all.

"Juniper, let's play at your house next time," said Clove. "I bet it's huge. Bet I could hide in your sock drawer. Bet your bathtub feels like a pool!"

Clove actually seemed to enjoy being small.

Juniper hadn't ever thought of it that way, but a cramp in her tail made it hard to focus on the idea.

The next day she returned to her way-too-big house. "Our home is very, nearly, almost perfect!" she said.

And while there were plenty of things
Juniper still didn't love about being little . . .

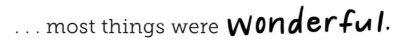

. . . most things were **wonderful.**